USBORNE PARANORMAL GUIDES

POLTERGEISTS?

Anna Claybourne

Designed by Stephen Wright
and Andy Dixon

Illustrated by Darrell Warner
and Gary Bines

Edited by Philippa Wingate
Consultants: John and Anne Spencer

Studio photography by Howard Allman
Digital images and textures created by John Russell
DTP by Michèle Busby
Additional illustrations by Jeremy Gower

Series Editor: Felicity Brooks

Picture research by Ruth King

CONTENTS

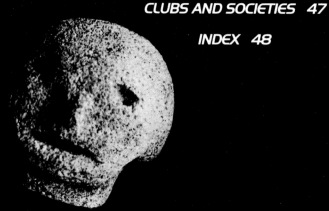

INTRODUCTION 3

Case study one: EERIE ENFIELD 4

THE FOCUS 10

Case study two: HAUNTED HYDESVILLE 12

Case study three: MOUNT RAINIER 16

POLTERGEISTS ON FILM 19

WHAT CAUSES POLTERGEISTS? 20

Case study four: PONTEFRACT PANIC 22

Case study five: MYSTERY ON MAN 28

HUNTING POLTERGEISTS 32

Case study six: SPIRITS OF BRAZIL 34

SPIRITS OF THE DEAD 39

Case study seven: THE HEXHAM HEADS 40

Case study eight: SPOOKY SAUCHIE 44

CLUBS AND SOCIETIES 47

INDEX 48

What are poltergeists?

Poltergeists are strange, invisible presences, often thought to be ghosts. Poltergeists haunt their victims by making loud noises and throwing things through the air. This is how they got their name – which is German for "noisy ghost".

Do they really exist?

Poltergeist cases have been reported for nearly 2,000 years, ever since the historian Titus Livius described stones being mysteriously hurled at Roman soldiers. In recent times, dozens of poltergeists have been reported all over the world – yet very few photographs have ever been taken of poltergeist disturbances.

Case studies

This book contains eight case studies. Each one tells the story of a poltergeist haunting, based on eyewitness accounts. Each case also includes an assessment, which examines the facts in an attempt to find out the truth behind the story.

You decide

To this day, poltergeists remain a mystery. In the end, it's for you to make up your own mind whether they exist. Even if they do, they usually seem to be harmless, and rarely hurt anyone badly.

This 16th-century woodcut, showing a demon pushing a man, is thought to be an attempt to illustrate a poltergeist haunting.

Case study one: EERIE ENFIELD

Date: August 31st, 1977
Place: Enfield, London, UK
Witnesses: Multiple witnesses

THE EVENTS

Janet Harper lay trembling in bed – but not with fear. It was the bed itself that was shaking. And she could hear strange shuffling noises, like footsteps. Janet and her brother Pete shouted for their mother, but then the shaking stopped.

The next night though, the family realized that something spooky *was* going on. The shaking returned, along with loud bangs. Then a heavy chest of drawers suddenly shuffled across the floor, all by itself. Terrified, the Harpers fled next door and called the police.

Chair scare

The policewoman who arrived, Officer Heeps, could not believe her eyes. A kitchen chair crept across the floor, as if pushed by an unseen hand.

The chair slowly rotated as it shuffled across the floor.

More mysteries

The police were baffled and could offer no explanation. Eventually, the Harpers had no choice but to move back home. However, over the next few weeks, more strange events occurred. Toys flew through the air, and were mysteriously hot to the touch. There were sudden cold breezes, and furniture lurched around, terrorizing the family.

Marbles and toy bricks flew through the air.

As the haunting continued, journalists and investigators from the Society for Psychical Research (see page 47) came to the house. One scientist was hit on the head by a toy brick. Janet was usually nearby when odd things occurred. Was she somehow connected to the poltergeist that was haunting her home?

Up in the air

After a while, Janet and her sister Rose began to be dragged out of bed by a strange force. Janet often fell asleep in her own bed, but woke up somewhere else.

David Robertson, a scientist, came to see if Janet was really levitating, which means defying gravity by floating through the air. Janet went into her room, and soon called out that she was flying. But when Robertson tried to go in, the door was stuck.

However, a milkman and an old woman, who had both been outside in the street at the time, reported something very odd. They said they had seen Janet through the window, floating in the air among a whirling mass of books and toys. The milkman, who had previously refused to believe gossip about the poltergeist, was petrified.

Main picture: One photograph appeared to show Janet floating through the air.

Above: Janet was photographed being hurled into the air.

Left: Janet's uncle found her asleep, balanced mysteriously on top of a large radio set.

Finding out more

A researcher named Maurice Grosse spent hours making notes of all the odd things he saw at the Harpers' house. These included small fires breaking out, and puddles appearing from nowhere.

The ghost speaks

Grosse tried talking to the poltergeist using rapping noises. The ghost was asked to make one rap for "no" and two for "yes", but its answers were confused. Then written messages started to appear. One read: "I WILL STAY IN THIS HOUSE."

Soon after that, the poltergeist appeared to speak in a deep, gruff man's voice, which seemed to be coming from Janet's throat.

A voice from the grave?

Janet claimed she had no control over the voice that spoke out of her mouth. It was much deeper and rougher than her normal voice. It was also rude, using lots of swear words. When questioned, the voice claimed to be the spirit of an old man who had died in the house years earlier. He told them he had died in a chair in the front room, and said that he threw Janet out of bed because it had been *his* bed when he was alive.

Was a poltergeist throwing toys around the house at Enfield?

During one of his conversations with the poltergeist, Maurice Grosse asked, "Are you playing games with me?"

As if in response to Grosse's question, a toybox flew through the air and hit him on the head.

There were many attempts to photograph the events at Enfield, but the poltergeist seemed camera-shy. Photographer Graham Morris found that his equipment repeatedly went wrong, and an expensive camera broke when Maurice Grosse took it into the house. A television reporter's tape recorder also mysteriously became jammed.

In the end, Morris did manage to take some photos that are still very hard to explain – unless there really *was* a poltergeist at work.

These two pictures, taken at one-second intervals, show a pillow that seems to be jumping and twisting by itself.

Teleportation

Teleportation is the name for something disappearing from one place and reappearing in another, often seeming to move through walls or other solid objects. One striking example of teleportation occured at Enfield. Mrs. Nottingham, who lived next door, found a book in her house. The book belonged to Janet, but it was on the other side of the wall from Janet's bedroom. No one had carried it there.

Another case of teleportation involved a boy who was haunted by a poltergeist.

One day, the boy was astonished to see his shirt fade away and vanish from his body.

The shirt which had disappeared was found hanging on a door in his house.

The Enfield poltergeist finally died away in 1978, more than a year after it appeared. It looks as if something paranormal, or supernatural, did happen. However, there is very little completely convincing evidence to prove beyond doubt that the Enfield house was haunted.

Was Enfield a hoax?

If so many strange things were really happening, why did it seem so hard to catch them on film?

Some investigators claim that the poltergeist didn't like to be recorded. Perhaps it avoided photographers and broke equipment deliberately, to avoid being filmed.

Others think this is just an excuse invented by the family to cover up their elaborate hoax.

Expert opinions

The investigators in the Enfield case had various disagreements. Maurice Grosse was sure he had experienced over 1,500 inexplicable events in the house. His colleague, Guy Lyon Playfair, also believed in the poltergeist and wrote a book about it.

Maurice Grosse reading *This House is Haunted* written by Guy Lyon Playfair

However, another investigator, Anita Gregory, said she never saw anything paranormal in the house. She said the children had told her to cover her face, while they giggled and faked the poltergeist-like events.

Recording equipment, including cameras and tape recorders, mysteriously stopped working in the Enfield house.

8

Focus on Janet

Janet was definitely the focus for the poltergeist (see page 10). Strange things almost always happened near her, or to her.

Some photographs show Janet's brothers and sisters looking upset, while she laughs or smiles. This might suggest she was playing tricks. But it is common in poltergeist cases for the focus to be unusually calm.

Years later Janet admitted she had sometimes tricked the investigators for fun. But she said most of the poltergeist's activities were real.

A speech therapist who studied the gruff voice said that Janet could have made it herself. If she had half-shut her epiglottis (which blocks your windpipe when you swallow) her voice would have sounded deep and rough.

Epiglottis —
Windpipe —

Other people in the street might have told Janet about the man who had lived in the house. Janet may have decided he seemed a fitting ghost.

Was she faking it?

Janet was photographed floating out of bed, but she could easily have jumped into the positions recorded in the photographs.

In this photograph, Janet (in the middle) is almost smiling, while Peter and Rose look less happy.

Still unexplained

Nevertheless, so many odd events were seen by so many witnesses that it's hard to believe they were all faked. To this day, the case remains a mystery.

THE FOCUS

Unlike ghosts, poltergeists usually seem to be linked to a particular living person. This person is known as the focus. In most cases, when objects fly around, doors slam or there are strange noises, the focus is almost always nearby.

Sometimes weird things happen to focuses too. They might find themselves being dragged out of bed or up a flight of stairs, or grabbed by invisible hands. They might go into a trance, or even levitate (float up into the air).

Despite this, the focus is rarely harmed, and the poltergeist usually disappears after a while.

Typical focuses

Focuses are usually young people aged between 11 and 16. Girls seem most likely to attract poltergeists.

A focus is often someone who is feeling upset or stressed. This might be caused by moving to a new house, by the focus's parents getting divorced, or just by the everyday pressures of being a teenager.

Above: Eleonore Zugun was the focus of an unusual poltergeist in the 1920s in Romania. Strange scratches appeared on her face.

Adults can also be focuses. One poltergeist in France picked on a young mother. Another haunted a 50-year-old man who worked at a gardening shop in Bromley, England. The shop became the scene of dozens of bizarre and scary events.

The Bromley poltergeist formed this frightening face in a mound of spilled fertilizer.

Can a focus cause a poltergeist?

Some experts think that focuses might even cause the odd occurrences that become known as poltergeist hauntings. It may be that some kind of mental energy, coming from the mind of the focus, is transformed into a physical force that can move objects and make noises.

Nobody really knows how this could happen. Most focuses don't *want* to be bothered by a poltergeist, and they certainly don't seem to cause hauntings deliberately.

So these strange mental powers, if they exist, must be subconscious. This means that the person who has them does not know about them, and can't control them.

Some investigators think that stress and worry, especially in teenagers, might somehow be expressed as a physical force.

This physical force could be the energy that causes objects to move by themselves or produces mysterious noises.

Case study two: HAUNTED HYDESVILLE

Date: March 31st, 1848
Place: Hydesville, New York, USA
Witnesses: Multiple witnesses

THE EVENTS

Mr. Michael Weekman never did find out what was causing the odd rumbling and shaking at his house in the village of Hydesville. Instead, he moved out, and Mr. and Mrs. Fox and their two youngest children moved in.

They had been there for only a few months when they began to hear the peculiar noises – thumping, banging and knocking. Night after night, the trouble continued.

At last the girls, Catherine, 12, and Margaretta, 14, were so unnerved that they started to sleep in the bed in their parents' bedroom.

Surprise replies

One Friday evening the family was in the bedroom and the odd noises were going on as usual. According to Mrs. Fox, Catherine suddenly shouted, "Mr. Splitfoot, do as I do!" Mr. Splitfoot was her name for the devil, and she was challenging the noise to copy her. She clapped her hands several times.

They waited. Then a rapping noise answered with exactly the same number of raps.

Now it was Margaretta's turn. She ordered the spirit, "Now, do as I do. Count one, two, three, four."

Back came the answer: rap, rap, rap, rap.

Margaretta and Catherine Fox, the sisters at the heart of the Hydesville haunting

Who are you?

Then Mrs. Fox decided to test the ghostly being. She asked it to rap out the ages of her seven children in order. It did so, getting all their ages exactly right.

Finally, it made three raps. These were for the youngest child of all, who had died at the age of three. Mrs. Fox shuddered. She was sure a dead spirit was present.

The family devised a code to ask the ghost questions. Spelling out answers, it told them it was the spirit of a salesman named Charles, who had been murdered in the house by having his throat cut. He said he was buried under the cellar floorboards.

The news spreads

News of the ghost spread through the village, and hundreds of people flocked to the house to witness the messages for themselves. Soon the newspapers picked up the story, and the Foxes became celebrities.

SPIRITUALISM
ORIGINATED MARCH 31ST 1848
IN THIS HOUSE

The Foxes' house now bears this sign.

The noises became linked to the two girls. When they moved to the town of Rochester, the rapping went too. The house at Hydesville was then haunted by gruesome gurgling noises. They sounded just like a man dying – from a slit throat.

Fame and fortune

Then the spirit told Catherine and Margaretta to hire a large hall and demonstrate the spooky messages to the public. The show was a great success, and the sisters went on tour. They amassed thousands of loyal followers. Many who witnessed their communication with the spirit believed that, at last, proof existed: there *was* life after death.

The Foxes' haunted house in Hydesville

Case study two: HAUNTED HYDESVILLE

Medium madness

Following the Fox sisters' success, talking to spirits became the height of fashion. The craze became known as Spiritualism. Suddenly there were hundreds of "mediums" – people who claimed they could contact the dead.

Mediums held "seances" – meetings where spirits were supposed to communicate with the living. Some mediums even said they could make ghosts appear, formed out of a strange white substance called ectoplasm. But ectoplasm was often faked using fine cloth or paper.

In this photograph, ectoplasm seems to materialize from a medium's ear.

"It's a fraud!"

In 1888, 40 years later, Margaretta called a public meeting. Crowds flocked to hear her, but they were astonished when she shouted, "It's a fraud! Spiritualism is a fraud from beginning to end!"

Margaretta said that she and her sister had faked the rapping noises by cracking joints in their toes. She stood on a table and demonstrated this with several loud knocks that echoed around the hall.

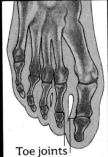

Toe joints

The sisters may have made rapping sounds by cracking their toe joints (shown in red).

A final twist

Surprisingly, many people would not believe Margaretta's confession, and Spiritualism continued as before. Then, three years later, Margaretta retracted her statement. She said the Catholic Church, which she had joined, had forced her to make a false confession rejecting Spiritualism.

Because of the huge media attention that surrounded the Fox sisters, it is very hard to tell what really went on in this case. Was Hydesville a hoax?

Could it be true?

It *is* possible that the sisters sometimes faked the noises with their toes. But that doesn't explain the shaking and banging in the Hydesville house at the start of the case, or the very loud knocking that hundreds of villagers witnessed.

Bones in the cellar

Was there any truth behind the spirit's story that a murdered salesman was buried in the cellar?

In 1904, some schoolchildren visiting the site of the Hydesville house found a skeleton under a wall that had collapsed. Nearby was a tin box of the type that salesmen carried long ago.

A skull and bones were found at Hydesville. Could they have belonged to a salesman?

Tried and tested

Early in their careers, the Fox sisters were subjected to rigorous tests by scientists. Most of these investigators ended up believing the sisters' claims.

Investigators said they had seen the Fox sisters make tables fly into the air.

A cunning combination?

Perhaps the case of the Fox sisters could be explained by a combination of trickery and real paranormal phenomena.

As the trend for Spiritualism took off, the sisters were under huge pressure to perform on the stage and in front of reporters. Because of this, they may have started to fake some of the rapping sounds.

But the early events, the shuffling, knocking and banging noises focusing on two girls, bear all the hallmarks of an unexplained poltergeist.

Case study three: MOUNT RAINIER

Date: 1949
Place: Mount Rainier,
Washington State, USA
Witnesses: The Mannheims

THE EVENTS

Robert Mannheim was fascinated by ghosts. His Aunt Harriet had taught him to use a Ouija board (see page 18), and 13-year-old Robert hoped that a dead spirit would use the board to send him a message from beyond the grave.

Holy shakes

One evening Robert's parents went out, leaving him at home with his grandmother. That was when a slow, scary dripping sound started echoing from one of the bedrooms. Robert and his grandmother ran to the room, and were shocked to see a painting of Jesus on the wall shaking violently – as if moved by an invisible hand. The room was also haunted by strange scratching noises.

A painting
of Jesus
shook eerily
to and fro.

It seemed as if a
ghostly hand was
moving the picture.

A death in the family

Just 11 days later, Aunt Harriet died, and Robert used his Ouija board to try to contact her spirit. On one occasion, the family heard footsteps in the haunted bedroom. Robert's mother called out, "Is that you, Harriet?"

She asked the spirit to make three knocks if it was Harriet. At once, three raps echoed around the room.

From then on, Robert became the victim of a poltergeist. Heavy objects were hurled around the house, and Robert was often dragged violently out of his chair onto the floor.

Scratched messages

The family tried sending Robert to stay with their priest, Reverend Schulze. But at Schulze's house, he was thrown out of a chair and under a bed. He soon came home.

Until then, the poltergeist had not been harmful. Now, something truly horrifying happened. Hideous scratches appeared on Robert's skin. They seemed to come, not from the outside of his body, but from the inside.

The scary scratches which appeared on Robert's body often spelled out words or his name.

Poltergeist possession?

Next, the ghostly presence spoke. A gravelly voice came from Robert's throat. Besides being much deeper than his own speech, sometimes the strange voice spoke in Latin – a language he didn't even know.

The Mannheims were terrified. Speaking in Latin is believed by the Catholic Church to be a sign of "possession" – when a demon takes over a person's body.

A Catholic cure

The Mannheims asked a priest to hold an "exorcism", a religious rite designed to banish evil spirits.

The haunting ended, and after his ordeal Robert became a Catholic. But can we be sure Robert was possessed? Was he pretending? Or was he the victim of a very clever poltergeist?

Equipment often used in exorcisms

In this engraving of an exorcism, demons are shown leaving a victim's body in a puff of smoke.

Case study three: THE ASSESSMENT

What caused Robert Mannheim's possession? No one is sure. But one thing is certain – Robert had a very active imagination. He was fascinated by ghosts, and he could have faked the scary voice for his own amusement. But the shaking picture, rapping and scratching are still a mystery. They would be much harder to fake.

Imitation?

Poltergeists seem to respond to what is happening around them. Perhaps Robert's poltergeist began to imitate a demon when possession was mentioned. Poltergeists often appear in cases of possession, so the two may be linked.

Exorcism – a cure?

Although exorcism helped Robert, that does not necessarily have to mean that he was really possessed by the devil or a demon. Instead, the prayers and rituals of the exorcism ceremony probably helped to calm him down. This may have made him feel that he had control over his strange situation, allowing him to overcome the problem by himself.

These old engravings show evil demons trying to attack people's souls with spears and arrows.

Ouija boards

Ouija (pronounced "weeja") boards, like the one Robert used, were invented during the 19th-century craze for talking to spirits.

Some people believed dead spirits could spell out messages by moving a pointer or an upturned glass around the letters of the alphabet, which were either painted on a board or printed on a set of cards.

However, to use a Ouija board, people had to put their hands on the pointer as it moved, so it was very easy for someone to cheat.

Letters   Pointer   Board

Spirits were thought to send messages by moving the pointer to different letters on a Ouija board.

POLTERGEISTS ON FILM

Surprisingly, although poltergeists are usually invisible, they have featured in several horror films.

Poltergeist

The *Poltergeist* films, made by Steven Spielberg in the 1980s, are the most famous of all poltergeist movies. They are not based on any one particular case. But they do feature most of the scary phenomena associated with poltergeists, including moving objects, bright lights, strange voices, people floating in the air, and ghostly apparitions.

A scene from the movie *Poltergeist*

Amityville

A series of movies was based on a haunting known as the Amityville horror. It began in 1975, when the Lutz family bought a house in Amityville, New York, USA. Before they moved in, a man had killed his family in the house.

The Lutzes left after doors started banging, Mrs. Lutz floated into the air, and green slime grew on the walls.

The Exorcist

The Exorcist (1973) was based on the Mount Rainier case (see page 16). The story was changed to make it more exciting. The film is about a priest who rids a girl of an evil spirit. Before she is cured, the girl vomits green slime and her head spins around.

WHAT CAUSES POLTERGEISTS?

Poltergeists are among the best-known paranormal phenomena. Dozens of cases from all over the world have been recorded, analyzed and investigated.

Yet, despite being so common, poltergeists are still very hard to explain. There are many different theories about what might cause them.

Medieval devils

In medieval times, people thought poltergeists were caused by devils or demons. It was believed that devils could possess people by living inside them, making them behave oddly, and speak in scary voices.

This demon appears in a book printed in 1631. It seems to be beckoning someone.

Power of the earth

We know there are powerful forces which we can't see, but which are perfectly natural. For example, radio waves are invisible but can travel long distances and carry signals. Magnets can make things move by an invisible force.

Some scientists think that poltergeists are caused by a similar kind of natural force, which can affect objects and people, but is not yet properly understood.

Someone who is a focus for a poltergeist may be sensitive to this force, just as people known as dowsers are sensitive to water.

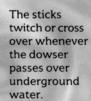

A dowser from a 1556 engraving

To find water, a modern dowser holds two sticks, called divining rods, loosely in both hands.

The sticks twitch or cross over whenever the dowser passes over underground water.

Scientists think that energy from the water may affect the dowser's body, making the rods move.

One theory suggests poltergeists are the spirits of dead people, trying to contact the world of the living from beyond the grave. Many poltergeists do seem to be intelligent. Some even identify themselves as dead spirits through voices or mess... unlike ghosts, polterge... focus on someone who... and fade away when th... becomes happier. So p... be caused by living hur...

Mind over matter

Many researchers think that poltergeists are in fact caused by the human mind itself in some way.

Some people do seem to be able to use mental energy to affect objects. For example, the performer Uri Geller claims to be able to bend items such as keys and spoons using his mind. This is called psychokinesis, or PK.

Poltergeists may in fact be a type of PK. In fact, poltergeist activity is often called RSPK (Recurrent Spontaneous Psychokinesis). "Recurrent" means repeated; "spontaneous" means the events happen by themselves.

Uri Geller bending a spoon by concentrating on it with his mind

Case study four: PONTEFRACT PANIC

Date: August, 1966
Place: Pontefract, England, UK
Witnesses: The Pritchard family

THE EVENTS

Marie clutched her husband Vic's hand. A chill ran down her spine as she, Vic and their friend Mr. O'Donald stepped into the dark hallway of her sister Jean Pritchard's haunted house.

Marie switched on a light, terrified of what she might see. But she saw nothing unusual.

Dust and water

However, something had certainly frightened Jean's son Phillip, aged 15, and his grand-mother, who were alone in the house. The rest of the family were away that week.

Earlier that night, Phillip had rushed across the road to Marie's house, saying that the living room was filled with strange white dust, and that there was water all over the floor.

Something strange

At first, Marie thought he must have gone crazy, but when she went to see for herself, she realized that Phillip was right. Something very strange indeed was going on.

In Jean Pritchard's house, Marie found a mysterious, fine white dust had settled all over the furniture in the living room.

A wardrobe began to move. It swayed and tottered like a drunken old man, terrifying the witnesses.

A plant pot was flung violently from the bottom of the stairs to the top, spilling soil everywhere.

Spooky response

Phillip and his grandmother went to stay at Marie's. But when Marie returned later with her husband and Mr. O'Donald, the house seemed to be back to normal. Mr. O'Donald, who knew about ghosts, told them that the Pritchards might have a poltergeist. He added that poltergeists often destroyed photographs.

The Pritchards' wedding photo was found mysteriously smashed.

After Mr. O'Donald had left, there was a loud crash. In the next room, a framed wedding photograph of Phillip's parents lay on the floor. The glass had been smashed, and the picture inside it had been slashed, as if with a sharp knife.

Goodbye... for now

That was the end of the haunting – for a time. When Phillip's family got home, there was no sign of anything odd. For a while, nothing strange or scary happened in the house.

The ghost returns

One afternoon, two years later, Jean Pritchard and her mother were having tea in the kitchen when they heard banging.

Jean was merely puzzled, but her mother looked nervous. Was the ghost back? Sure enough, what they saw bore all the signs of the strange visitor that had haunted the house two years earlier.

A pot plant was upturned on the carpet, and a blanket had been thrown to the bottom of the stairs.

This time, however, the spook was here to stay...

Case study four: PONTEFRACT PANIC

Before long, the Pritchards' house became nightmarish to live in. There were constant banging and crashing noises. The family had objects thrown at them, and huge teeth marks appeared in food that had been left in the refrigerator.

A paintbrush which was being used to paint a bedroom was flung through the air.

In one room, which was being decorated, a roll of wallpaper stood on its end, swaying like a cobra.

The poltergeist seemed to focus on Diane, Phillip's younger sister. She was thrown out of bed several times, and dragged up the stairs by her cardigan.

Diane was dragged by an invisible hand.

Candlestick chiller

Eventually, the frightened family called in a priest to see if he could help. The clergyman was cynical. He told the Pritchards he didn't believe their stories. If their furniture was moving, he said, it must be caused by the ground subsiding, or caving in, under the house.

At once, as if to prove him wrong, a candlestick floated into the air under his nose, and hovered there. That soon changed the minister's mind. He left, saying there was evil in the house.

A candlestick seemed to wave itself deliberately in the priest's face.

Aunt Maude comes to stay

Diane's and Phillip's Aunt Maude, the sister of their father Joe, didn't believe a word of the poltergeist stories. She thought the children were just playing tricks. So she came to see for herself.

When Maude arrived, all the lights went out. The refrigerator door flew open, and a jug of milk floated out. It crossed the room and poured milk all over Aunt Maude's head!

But Maude still wasn't convinced. She decided to stay the night.

A sleepless night

The night Aunt Maude spent in the house was one of the scariest so far. Crashing noises kept everyone awake; the doors banged, and the entire contents of the refrigerator were flung across the kitchen floor. Then lightbulbs from a room downstairs appeared in the bedroom where Diane, her mother and Aunt Maude were trying to sleep.

Haunting hands

Aunt Maude couldn't deny that something very odd was happening when a lamp floated across the room, all by itself. Then, suddenly, two enormous, hairy hands reached around the half-closed bedroom door. One was at the top, and one near the bottom, so that it looked as if there was a huge monster behind the door. The hands were Aunt Maude's fur gloves, moving by themselves!

Tune tease

Maude shouted, "Get away – you're evil!" One glove shook its fist at her. Maude then began to sing a hymn to scare the evil away, but the gloves simply beat time to the tune.

Jean Pritchard later admitted that although she was frightened, she had had to smile at the way the ghost was teasing Aunt Maude.

Case study four: PONTEFRACT PANIC

Menacing monk

At first, the poltergeist that tormented the Pritchard family was invisible. But one night, when Jean and Joe were in bed, their door swung open. There, in the shadows, lurked a tall, cloaked figure. When they switched on the light, it vanished.

Several local people said they had seen the figure too. One said the ghostly shape looked like a monk.

This map shows the location of the Pritchards' house, and the site of the ancient Cluniac monastery that had once stood nearby.

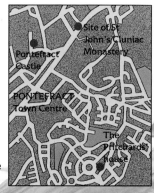

Vengeful ghost

The Pritchards had recently found out that their house was near the site of an old monastery which had been destroyed in the 16th century.

A local woman thought she might have an explanation for the haunting. She said she remembered reading about a monk from the monastery who had been hanged for attacking a woman. Could his spirit still be wandering the Earth, tormenting local people to take revenge?

The monk appears... and disappears

One day, Phillip and Diane were watching TV when they suddenly saw the monk through a glass door.

Phillip ran over to the door, trying to get a better view of the figure. But as he opened the door, the ghost fled.

Phillip just managed to see the monk disappear through the kitchen floor. After that, it was never seen again.

Case study four: THE ASSESSMENT

Is it possible that, as Aunt Maude first thought, the Pritchard children were playing tricks?

The Pontefract poltergeist was one of the most mischievous ever known. It liked to tease people, which might make it seem like a hoax. However, other poltergeists have been known to tease their victims.

A new focus?

It is very unusual for the same family to have a poltergeist twice. Did a ghost really visit the Pritchards on two different occasions, over a period of two whole years?

The first haunting began when Phillip was 15. The ghost returned when Diane was 14. These are both typical ages for a poltergeist victim. Experts might say that the two teenagers in turn became focuses (see page 10) for a poltergeist.

Was it a monk?

A researcher, Colin Wilson, tried to track down the story of the hanged monk. The Pritchards' friend was sure she had read all about it at the local library.

But Wilson found no evidence that a monk had ever been hanged in the area. In fact, the monk story seems to have been no more than hearsay, developed into a theory by the Pritchards and their friends.

Seeing things

Apparitions, or visible ghosts, do sometimes occur in poltergeist cases. But that doesn't mean the Pritchards were being haunted by the ghost of a monk.

The Pontefract poltergeist often seemed to respond to suggestions. For example, the photograph was smashed just after Mr. O'Donald had mentioned photos.

Perhaps, if there really was a poltergeist, it responded to the family's expectations by appearing in the form of a ghost.

No answer

Many aspects of this case still baffle researchers. No one has ever explained how Maude's gloves became scary hands, or how objects in the house moved by themselves.

A Cluniac monk of the type who had lived near to the site of the Pritchards' house

Case study five: MYSTERY ON MAN

Date: September, 1931
Place: Isle of Man, UK
Witnesses: The Irving family

THE EVENTS

Mr. Irving peered up into the dank gloom of the attic.

There it was again! The scratching, snuffling noise that had puzzled the family for days was getting louder. It was joined by hissing sounds.

Mr. Irving had decided that a small creature – a rat or a squirrel – must be trapped up there.

But he could see nothing.

He went back downstairs to join his wife and 13-year-old daughter, Voirrey. Suddenly, a massive "CRACK!" shook the walls, and made everyone jump.

Weird weasel

Over the next few days, all three Irvings thought they caught glimpses of an odd animal, similar to a weasel, around the house. It was yellow and about the size of a large rat.

Mr. Irving even tried making animal noises, which the creature repeated.

Word for word

One evening in November, Mr. Irving jokingly tried singing a short nursery rhyme instead of making the animal noises. His blood ran cold as he heard the creature's uncanny, high-pitched voice repeat every single word – just as he had sung it.

Mr. Irving searched the attic for the mysterious creature.

Squeaking and speaking

Gradually, the strange voice began to sound more human. It stopped imitating, and talked about itself.

The voice said that it belonged to the spirit of a mongoose – a type of small, weasel-like animal – that had lived in India in the 1850s. It even gave itself a name: Gef.

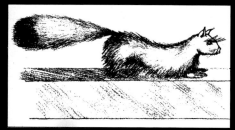

This sketch of Gef was drawn by a local newspaper reporter, following the family's own description of their talking mongoose.

Mongoose on the loose

Although the family believed that Gef was an animal, what happened in the next few days strongly resembled the work of a poltergeist.

As well as the strange voice, loud noises filled the house. Stones appeared out of thin air, and the Irvings were horrified to see plates and dishes moving by themselves.

One farmworker had a particularly terrifying experience. He threw a crust of bread on the ground, and then saw it rise into the air and float away – just as if it were being carried by a small, invisible creature.

Gef and Voirrey

Voirrey seemed to be a particular target. She had stones thrown at her, which is a typical poltergeist activity, and Gef's voice swore at her. She moved into her parents' bedroom to escape the piercing, shrieking voice. But Gef could be heard snarling, "I'll follow her, wherever you move her!"

Strangely, however, Gef had a lot in common with Voirrey. A clever but lonely girl, she had a great interest in mechanical things. Gef, too, talked about machines and technology.

Voirrey was also good at catching rabbits – and Gef often left rabbits in the house as presents for the family.

The Isle of Man, off the coast of England

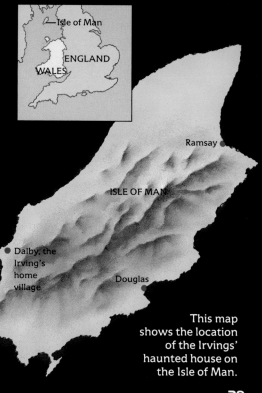

This map shows the location of the Irvings' haunted house on the Isle of Man.

In the news

The story of the mysterious talking mongoose spread far and wide, and investigators began to arrive at the Irvings' remote house.

A reporter from a newspaper, The *Daily Dispatch*, was one of the few people outside the family to hear Gef speak. He was baffled by the piercing, uncanny voice of the talking mongoose. But he also began to suspect that there was a connection between Gef and Voirrey. He wondered if she might be making the voice herself, but he was unable to prove this for certain.

Dog hair doubts

Two researchers eventually turned up at the house with a camera, hoping to find proof that the talking mongoose existed.

Voirrey and her dog, Mona, whose fur was used to test the Irvings' claims.

While Gef spoke, the reporter watched Voirrey's reflection in a mirror. To his frustration, she partly covered her mouth with her hand.

During the researchers' stay, Gef was neither seen nor heard. But they didn't leave empty-handed. They secretly clipped a tuft of hair from the family dog. They also left the camera so that Voirrey could photograph Gef, and asked her, if possible, to send a clipping of Gef's fur to their London office. Eventually a clipping arrived. Under the microscope, it matched exactly the dog fur they had taken.

Case study five: THE ASSESSMENT

Many years later, the bizarre events on the Isle of Man still intrigue experts. Was Voirrey Irving the focus for a very unusual poltergeist? Or did she somehow fake the haunting?

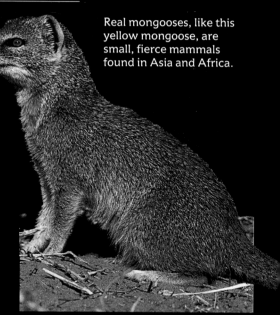

Real mongooses, like this yellow mongoose, are small, fierce mammals found in Asia and Africa.

All a hoax?

Gef could have been a joke played by the teenaged Voirrey – perhaps to relieve her boredom. His high-pitched voice, though odd, could have been made by a girl. Gef was only active when Voirrey was nearby, and no one outside the family saw him. The way Voirrey hid her mouth from the reporter is especially suspicious.

The lonely farmhouse on the Isle of Man where Voirrey and her parents lived

Poltergeist mongoose?

Yet much is still unexplained. Even if the voice was Voirrey's, flying objects and stones are harder to fake. These events are typical of other poltergeist cases. In addition poltergeists often seem to focus on girls of Voirrey's age (see page 10).

Fake fur

Why did the Irvings try to convince investigators by sending them a clipping of dog fur? This seems to point to obvious trickery.

But it doesn't necessarily rule out a poltergeist. Poltergeists have often been known to avoid investigators and refuse to perform for the cameras. This can lead to witnesses being ridiculed.

Sending the tuft of dog hair could have been a desperate attempt to get someone to take the haunting seriously.

The clipping of dog fur sent to the investigators

HUNTING POLTERGEISTS

When a house or other building shows signs of having a poltergeist, investigators may be called in to discover exactly what is happening. Is it a hoax? Are the victims imagining everything? Or is something truly strange going on?

The sleuths use a range of methods to try to find out. It's not an easy task, as poltergeists are notorious for avoiding detection.

Sneaky spooks

Poltergeists often seem to know they are being watched, and avoid their activities being recorded.

This could mean that most reports of poltergeists are really just hoaxes. On the other hand, poltergeists may in fact be caused by some kind of natural force (see page 20), which could interfere with electrical equipment and stop it from working.

Taking poltergeist pictures

A genuine photograph or video of objects flying through the air would be the best proof that poltergeists really do exist. Strangely, however, researchers have found it almost impossible to photograph or film objects moving by themselves or appearing from nowhere. This even occurs in cases in which the witnesses involved in the hauntings swear they have seen these things happening. Often, cameras are mysteriously damaged, or malfunction just as the paranormal events begin.

In one case, witnesses claimed that objects in a house in Hertfordshire, UK, mysteriously moved.

Investigators set up a video camera and left it running in the house; but it recorded nothing.

But 15 minutes after the camera's tape ran out, witnesses claimed things began moving again.

The equipment used by spook detectives

Poltergeist researchers sometimes use a machine called an EMU (Environmental Monitoring Unit). This tests factors such as air movements and temperature. Left in a haunted house, the EMU records changes in the atmosphere that might indicate a strange presence. For example, many witnesses claim that ghosts make the air cold. So a sudden chill could indicate a spook. EMUs also detect voices, footsteps and warmth from a human body, so researchers can tell if an "empty" room is visited by a hoaxer.

An EMU in use at a haunted site

This diagram shows how an EMU (Environmental Monitoring Unit) works.

Microphone

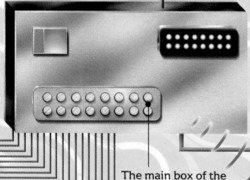

Different sensors measure various signals, such as vibrations, temperature changes and air movements.

Temperature sensor

The main box of the EMU has 16 switches which activate various sensors.

Radio signals

Wires lead from the EMU to 16 sensors placed in different parts of the site being investigated.

The EMU's data is sent by radio signal to a computer, which records and analyzes it.

On record

If a poltergeist is suspected, investigators often ask victims to keep a log, recording the date, time and nature of each eerie event.

Then the log is analyzed, and researchers can look for patterns. For example, they might notice that the ghost is only active when a particular person is present.

Sugar trap

Like cameras, EMUs often stop working in haunted houses. Sometimes researchers resort to traditional detective tricks. For example, a little sugar on a floor shows footprints if someone has walked through a room.

Case study six: SPIRITS OF BRAZIL

Brazil, in South America, is one of the world's most haunted countries. Here is a selection of mysterious events that have happened there.

> **Case: A POLTERGEIST IN GUARULHOS**
> **Date: April 27th, 1973**
> **Place: Guarulhos, Sao Paulo, Brazil**
> **Witnesses: Multiple witnesses**

THE EVENTS

Noemia was furious. Someone, or something, had carved four long, deep slashes into one of the mattresses in her house.

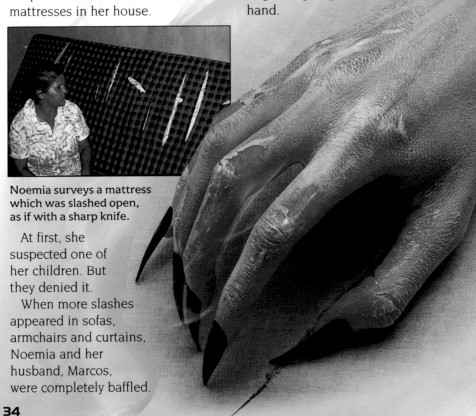

Noemia surveys a mattress which was slashed open, as if with a sharp knife.

At first, she suspected one of her children. But they denied it.

When more slashes appeared in sofas, armchairs and curtains, Noemia and her husband, Marcos, were completely baffled.

Invisible blades

One day, three members of the family were together in a bedroom. They stared in horror as, before their eyes, deep cuts appeared in one of the beds.

Monster claw

The next strange experience happened to Pedro, Marcos's father. He was terrified when a monstrous arm appeared before him in the air. Its long, razor-sharp claws reached threateningly toward his face.

A friend visited to see what was going on – but fainted in fright when she saw a huge, long-fingered hand.

Did the fierce claws that Pedro saw slash the furniture?

Face fright

A few days later, Noemia had another terrifying experience. She had seen vague shapes and shadows before, but this time she clearly caught sight of a grotesque face, with huge fangs, surrounded by flickering flames. Soon afterward, fires started in the house.

No escape

The evil force followed the petrified family from place to place. They moved six times in an attempt to escape – and each time the poltergeist came with them. It only left in October 1976, after an exorcism (see page 17) was held.

In the flesh

The worst was yet to come. Soon, the ghost began to attack people. One day, Marcos woke in agonizing pain. He looked down in horror at his arm. It was slashed open and bleeding.

Noemia too was attacked by an invisible presence. Feeling a sudden pain, she looked in the mirror and found tiny, sharp cuts on her face and neck.

This map shows the sites in Brazil described in these case studies.

Case: FIRES IN RAMOS
Date: 1989
Place: Ramos, Brazil
Witnesses: Multiple witnesses

THE EVENTS

Sara shrank back in terror. A hideous devil was looming over her, leering and pointing. Laughing evilly, he promised to burn her to death. Sara screamed and buried her face in the bedclothes.

A fiery devil haunted Sara in her dreams.

She ran to her grandmother's room, still tormented by her nightmare. When they returned to Sara's bedroom, they froze. The bed was covered in black scorch marks. Someone had tried to start a fire.

Flaring up

The trouble had started the day before. After an argument with her grandmother, several small fires had broken out, always near 13-year-old Sara. At first it seemed to be a coincidence.

Explosive

After Sara's nightmare, however, the fires got worse. A mattress, a bundle of clothes and even a damp towel caught fire with loud explosions. A priest advised the terrified girl to leave the house. She went to stay with a friend, and the fires stopped – but they returned as soon as she did.

Cured with kindness

At last, Sara moved in with a kind woman next door, Mrs. de Sousa, and the trouble ended as quickly as it had begun. It seemed to have been caused by the bad relationship between Sara and her grandmother.

Could the fires have been started by a poltergeist, expressing Sara's emotions with explosive force?

Sara and her grandmother were scared by the mysterious burns on the bed.

Case: JABUTICABAL
Date: December, 1965
Place: Jabuticabal, Brazil
Witnesses: Multiple witnesses

THE EVENTS

It had been a terrible night for 11-year-old Maria. She had woken several times, terrified and unable to breathe.

When she awoke in the night, Maria found her pillow pressing down on her face. It was as if someone was trying to suffocate her.

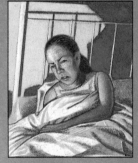

When morning came, and Maria woke again, this time in agony. The pillow wasn't suffocating her, but her arm felt very sore.

Looking down at her arm, Maria was horrified to see that dozens of small sewing needles had been stuck painfully into her flesh.

Ghostly gifts

The haunting had started when falling bricks had appeared from nowhere. Instead of being afraid, Maria accepted the events, and even asked the ghost for presents. If she requested food, it would appear. Once, she asked for a brooch. It appeared at her feet.

Revenge of the dead?

Then the spirit stopped being so friendly. Maria was slapped and bitten, and the nocturnal attacks began.

A friend, Volpe, took Maria to a Spiritualist club, where mediums tried to contact the ghost.

A medium from Brazil

Volpe watched, amazed, as an eerie spirit voice spoke from Maria's throat. In a past life, it said, Maria had been a witch. Now, the ghost of one of her victims was taking its revenge.

A sticky end

Several years later, Maria drank a soft drink which had been laced with poison. She died that day. Was it suicide? Or had a ghost poisoned her, as a last act of vengeance?

Case study six: THE ASSESSMENT

The poltergeists of Brazil certainly seem to have scared those who experienced them. But many of these odd and disturbing cases could have a rational explanation.

Monsters in the mind

In the Guarulhos case, Pedro was sure he had seen a hideous claw. But he could have imagined it. Perhaps his mind created an image of a creature that could have made the slashes in the furniture. No one else saw the same claw. Pedro's story could then have scared the other occupants of the house into imagining that they too could see horrible monsters.

Poltergeist poisoning

Did a ghost really poison Maria in the Jabuticabal case? It may seem unlikely. But perhaps ghostly poisoning *is* possible. There is a case in which a spirit known as the "Bell Witch" haunted the Bell family in the USA in 1817. The witch claimed to have killed the father of the family, John Bell. It said it had replaced his medicine bottle with a flask full of poisonous liquid. After drinking it, Bell died.

Spontaneous fires

Fires have often been reported in poltergeist cases, although they usually do very little damage.

Perhaps the fires that plagued 13-year-old Sara at Ramos were linked to another type of paranormal event, called Spontaneous Human Combustion, or SHC.

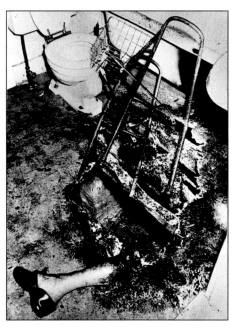

A leg was all that was left of Dr. J. Irving Bentley after he mysteriously burst into flames in his bathroom.

In cases of SHC, people themselves burst into flames, without an obvious cause. In Sara's case, however, fires seemed to burn *around* her, but she was unharmed.

Scientists are still trying to explain SHC. Meanwhile, the cause of Sara's spontaneous fires remains a mystery.

Could poltergeists be dead spirits, returning to Earth to take revenge, or torment people for fun? After all, they seem to use rapping, messages or voices to reveal an identity from beyond the grave.

I WILL STAY IN THIS HOUSE

Messages, such as this one from Enfield (see page 4), sometimes appear in poltergeist cases.

Questions and answers

Researchers have found that poltergeists often do exactly what observers expect. If people ask them questions they frequently reply. But this doesn't mean poltergeists are dead spirits. They could be caused by the human mind – or they could be hoaxes.

Days of the Dead

In many Latin American countries, people hold a celebration for the dead each November. Families prepare feasts for dead relatives and friends and make model skulls and skeletons.

The celebrations are happy and festive, not scary. But they do reveal a strong belief in dead spirits in Latin America.

Skeletons, candles and flowers decorate homes.

Decorations based on the theme of skeletons and witches

This may be why so many ghosts and poltergeists are reported there. If more people believe in ghosts, they are more likely to put unexplained events down to ghostly spirits.

Date: February, 1972
Place: Hexham, England, UK
Witnesses: Multiple witnesses

The heads seemed to have been carved from some kind of heavy stone.

THE EVENTS

Can a poltergeist be triggered by an ancient curse?

That's what seemed to happen after 11-year-old Colin Robson found a curious object buried outside his house. When he brushed away the dirt, he saw that it was a small carved stone head, about 5cm (2in) across. He called his brother Leslie to come and look, and Leslie found a second head. The boys took their finds inside to show their parents.

The weirdness begins

That was when disturbing events, similar to a poltergeist haunting, began to happen. Objects in the house started to move – including the heads themselves, which would spin around and around. Eerie lights glowed on the lawn at night. Several items were found broken, and a shower of broken glass landed on an empty bed.

The "boy" head had a long nose and a broad face.

The "girl" head was small and had a pointed nose and chin.

Shattered glass was found on an empty bed.

Creature shock

Soon, the scary events spread to next door, where 10-year-old Brian Dodd was ill in bed. His mother, Ellen, was looking after him.

As Brian lay in bed, he became jumpy and nervous. He complained that he could feel something very strange touching him on his legs.

Then, to her horror, Mrs. Dodd saw a werewolf-like creature creep across the bedroom floor. It looked half human and half animal.

The monster crawled nearer and nearer, and Mrs. Dodd froze in fear as it pawed her leg. Then it padded out of the room.

An expert takes over

The monster upset the Dodd family so much that they moved out. The Robsons also left home for a while.

The heads were sent to the home of Dr. Anne Ross, an expert in ancient tribes. She believed the heads had been made by the Celts, a race of people who lived in Britain almost 2,000 years ago.

Night fright

Dr. Ross was used to old carvings. They didn't scare her. Yet spooky things soon began happening to her too. One night she woke up suddenly. She was freezing cold, and very scared. By the door stood a monstrous figure. Its lower half was human, but its top half was covered in dark fur. It had a wolf's head.

Dr. Ross chased the monster downstairs, but it disappeared. Later, her daughter saw the werewolf, and the house was plagued by crashing sounds. Yet, as soon as the heads were taken away, the haunting stopped.

The monster stood about 2m (7ft) tall.

A Celtic curse

Dr. Ross's family were sure the Hexham heads had caused the trouble. Even her husband sensed an evil presence, although he did not normally believe in such things.

Perhaps the Celts had made the heads, and bewitched them with a curse. After all, many Celtic tribes believed heads were very powerful, and stone heads played an important part in Celtic religious rituals.

Stone heads like this one, the Hendy Head, were made by the Celts, and used in religious ceremonies.

"I made them!"

Dr. Ross believed the heads were Celtic. But there was a surprise in store when a truck driver called Desmond Craigie told his story:

Craigie said he had lived in the Robsons' house before they moved in. He had a job making pillars out of cement.

One day in 1956 – just 16 years earlier – he had made the Hexham heads in his lunch hour, as a present for his young daughter.

The heads must have been lost outside the house, where the Robson boys later found them. They weren't really ancient after all.

If this were true, what caused all the strange events and the appearance of the terrifying werewolf? New or old, the heads did seem to have some kind of paranormal power.

Today, the heads have again been lost. Whoever finds them might once more unleash those evil forces.

Case study seven: THE ASSESSMENT

Could the Hexham case have been caused by a poltergeist? It's possible. In both Robson and Ross households, there were children who could have acted as a focus. Objects moved about, and there were strange noises and temperature changes. Even the werewolf might have been poltergeist-related. Apparitions – ghostly figures – are rare, but not unheard of, in poltergeist cases.

Weird imaginings

Another possibility is that the haunting was imagined. The families may have discussed curses and horror stories, and convinced themselves that they had seen something scary in the night.

The werewolf – half man, half beast – has existed for a long time in popular legend.

But Dr. Ross was not the kind of person to let her imagination run wild. Also, why did different people's descriptions of the creature match each other so closely?

A new theory

Another scientist, Dr. Don Robins, also studied the Hexham heads and found they contained a mineral called quartz. Under a microscope, quartz has a regular, grid-like chemical structure.

A crystal of quartz

Dr. Robins thought that this structure might be able to store images, in the same way as a computer stores information in the form of numbers. A lump of quartz might, for example, be able to hold a "recording" of an event.

The presence of the heads, Dr. Robins suggested, could then have caused these stored images, such as the werewolf creature, to appear.

A spooky feeling

Even if Dr. Robins's idea is right, scientists don't yet know how it works. But one thing is certain; even Dr. Robins, whose theory should have made him feel safe, was scared of the heads, and didn't like having them in his house.

Case study eight: SPOOKY SAUCHIE

Date: November 22nd, 1960
Place: Sauchie, Scotland, UK
Witnesses: Multiple witnesses

THE EVENTS

Terrified, Virginia and Margaret huddled together as the strange noise came closer and closer. It sounded exactly like a large ball being bounced all around their bed. Their eyes darted fearfully around the room; but, apart from the two girls, the bedroom was empty.

The bizarre noise sounded as if an invisible person were bouncing an invisible ball around the bed.

Automatic doors

A few days later, Virginia was alone in the house. As she approached one of the old wooden doors, she felt a strange chill. She took another step. With a slow creak, the door opened. At first she thought it was the wind. But as she walked on, door after door opened unaided, and when she tried to shut them, they were stuck fast.

Signs of a poltergeist

Later, Virginia was astonished to see a heavy wooden cupboard suddenly slide a short distance away from the wall. Just as quickly, it slid back.

After that, other objects such as chairs, crockery and fruit, began to move around by themselves, in full view of the whole family.

An apple floating out of a fruit bowl was one of the many strange sights reported in the Sauchie case.

A new home

Virginia and her mother were staying with relatives in the Scottish village of Sauchie. They had just left their home in Ireland, and Virginia wasn't happy. She missed her father and her dog, Toby, who had remained in Ireland.

An invisible head

The rest of the village soon heard about the haunting. A local priest and three doctors came to hear the bouncing ball noise for themselves, as Virginia lay in bed. Then, as the stunned visitors stared, the bedclothes began to ripple unnaturally, and loud scratching and banging noises filled the room.

Virginia trembled under the covers. But she was not harmed. Instead, an indentation, the size and shape of a human head, slowly pressed itself into her pillow.

The impression of a head appeared in Virginia's pillow.

Cups, plates and dishes, seemed to move by themselves.

It followed her to school

Strange things soon started to happen at Virginia's school as well, amazing her teacher, Miss Stewart.

One day, Miss Stewart saw Virginia desperately trying to hold down her desk lid. It seemed to want to open by itself.

The girl who sat in front of Virginia got up and left her place to go to Miss Stewart's desk.

Then, in full view of everyone, a desk slowly rose up off the ground and floated in the air.

The table turns

On another occasion, Virginia was standing by Miss Stewart's heavy oak table. A wooden pointer on the table began to vibrate, and the table floated into the air and slowly rotated. But Miss Stewart wasn't afraid. She said there was no ghost and nothing to fear. Soon after that, the haunting stopped.

Case study eight: THE ASSESSMENT

Although not the scariest or most spectacular of poltergeist hauntings, the Sauchie case is one of the most convincing on record.

Eyewitness evidence
In many poltergeist cases, it is possible to put the haunting down to a hoax, exaggeration, or overactive imaginations. But in Sauchie, spooky events were witnessed and agreed upon by several reliable observers.

The priest, the doctors and the teacher were all adults with responsible jobs. They would have had nothing to gain by making up ghost stories. This suggests they really did witness something they couldn't explain.

Sauchie, in Scotland, where a poltergeist allegedly struck

Classic case
Virginia was a typical focus for a poltergeist. She was 11 years old; she had recently moved to a new house, and she might have been depressed. All these things made her a classic poltergeist victim.

When Virginia had settled down in her new home, the strange events faded away, indicating that the haunting could have been caused by her disturbed state of mind.

The bouncing ball noise heard at Sauchie was experienced by many witnesses. Their descriptions of the sound all matched exactly.

A likely story?
As with many poltergeist stories, there is no firm evidence, such as a film, to prove that anything strange happened at Sauchie.

Yet a number of people who were involved in the case still say they saw something very odd indeed. And the reliability of the witnesses suggests that this unexplained case could have an element of truth.

CLUBS AND SOCIETIES

Many societies have been formed to study, discuss and investigate weird and wonderful phenomena. You can write to some of them for information and help with hobbies or school projects.

The SPR

In the 1870s, the craze for trying to contact dead spirits was at its height. Hypnosis and telepathy (a way of communicating using only the mind) were very fashionable.

At around this time, a group of scientists and scholars in London, England decided to form a society to study strange phenomena. In 1882, the Society for Psychical Research, or SPR, was born.

The SPR still exists today. Instead of trying to prove or disprove paranormal events, it aims to find out as much about them as possible.

More reading

Magazines such as *Fortean Times* and *Fate* cover all kinds of strange, spooky and scary phenomena. As well as poltergeists, they report on ghosts, magic, telepathy and other wonders. If you can't find them for sale locally, you could send off for a subscription to one of the addresses shown below.

Fortean Times magazine

Addresses

Here are some addresses to write to. These organizations and magazines may also be able to put you in touch with a club or society in your own area.

The Society for Psychical Research
49 Marloes Road
London W8 6LA,
England, UK

The American Society for
Psychical Research
5 West 73rd Street
New York, NY 10023, USA

Fate Magazine
Llewellyn Worldwide Ltd
P.O. Box 64383
St. Paul, MN 55164-0383, USA

Fortean Times
The New Boathouse
136-142 Bramley Road
London W10 6SR, England, UK

INDEX

American Society for Psychical Research, 47
Amityville, 19
apparitions, 19, 27, 43

Bell Witch, 38
Brazilian cases, 34-38
Bromley poltergeist, 10

cameras, 7, 8, 30, 31, 32, 33
Catholic Church, 14, 17
Celts, 41, 42
Craigie, Desmond, 42
curses, 40, 42

Days of the Dead, 39
dead spirits, 13, 16, 21, 26, 39, 47
demons, 3, 17, 18, 20
devils, 18, 20
divining rods, 20
dowsers, 20

ectoplasm, 14
Enfield case, 4-9, 39
Environmental Monitoring Unit (EMU), 33
exorcism, 17, 18, 35
The Exorcist, 19

Fate magazine, 47
films, 19
fires, 6, 35, 36, 38

focuses, 9, 10-11, 15, 20, 27, 31, 43, 46
Fortean Times, 47
Fox sisters, 12-15

Gef, 29-31
Geller, Uri, 21
ghosts, 3, 10, 14, 16, 17, 18, 21, 25, 26, 33, 35, 37, 38, 39, 45, 46, 47
Gregory, Anita, 8
Grosse, Maurice, 6, 7, 8
Guarulhos case, 34, 35, 38

Harper, Janet and family, 4-9
Hexham heads, 40-43
hoaxing, 8, 14, 15, 18, 27, 31, 32, 33, 39, 46
horror films, 19
Hydesville case, 12-15
hypnosis, 47

investigators, 4, 8, 9, 11, 15, 31, 32, 47
Isle of Man case, 28-31
Irving family, 28-31

Jabuticabal case, 35, 37, 38

levitating, 5, 10

magnets, 20
Mannheim, Robert and

family, 16-18
mediums, 14
mental energy, 11, 21
messages, 6, 13, 16, 18, 21, 39
mongooses, 29, 30, 31
monks, 26, 27
monsters, 38, 41
Mount Rainier case, 16-18, 19
movies, 19

newspapers, 13, 30

Ouija boards, 16, 17, 18

paranormal, 8, 15, 20, 32, 42, 47
photographs, 3, 5, 7, 8, 9, 23, 32
Playfair, Guy Lyon, 8
poisoning, 37, 38
Poltergeist, 19
Pontefract case, 22-27
possession, 17, 18, 20
priests, 17, 24, 36, 45, 46
Pritchard family, 22-27
psychokinesis (PK), 21

quartz, 43

radio waves, 20
Ramos case, 35, 36, 38
rapping, 6, 12, 13, 15, 39
recurrent spontaneous

psychokinesis (RSPK), 21
reporters, 4, 15, 30, 31
researchers, 6, 30
Robertson, David, 5
Robins, Dr. Don, 43
Robson family, 40-43
Ross, Dr. Anne, 41-43

Sauchie case, 44-46
scientists, 4, 5, 15, 20, 43, 47
seances, 14
Society for Psychical Research (SPR), 4, 47
spirits, 6, 13, 14, 16, 17, 18, 19, 21, 26, 37, 39, 47
Spiritualism, 13, 14
spontaneous human combustion (SHC), 38
stress, 10, 11

telepathy, 47
teleportation, 7

voices, 6, 9, 17, 18, 19, 21, 28, 29, 30, 31, 37, 39

werewolves, 41, 42, 43
Wilson, Colin, 27
witches, 37, 38, 39

Zugun, Eleonore, 10

Every effort has been made to trace the copyright holders of the material in this book. If any rights have been omitted, the publishers offer to rectify this in any subsquent editions following notification. The publishers are grateful to the following organizations and individuals for their permission to reproduce material: (t=top, b=bottom, r=right, l=left)

p2 Paul Screeton/Fortean Picture Library; p3 Bodleian Library: Von Bruder Rauschen, 1835, title-page woodcut; p4-5 Graham Morris; p5 (bl) Graham Morris; p5 (br) Graham Morris; p6-7 Comstock 1998; p7 (tr) both Mirror Syndication International; p8 (tr) Maurice Grosse; p8 (bl) photographed with thanks to Olympus Cameras; p9 (b) Mirror Syndication International; p10 (tr) Fortean Picture Library; p14 (bl) Fortean Picture Library; p15 (tr) Fortean Picture Library; p16 Ecce Homo by Vicente Juan Macip (Juan de Juanes) (c. 1510-79), Prado, Madrid/Bridgeman Art Library, London/New York; p17 (br) Fortean Picture Library; p18 (br) Images Colour Library; p19 (b) MGM2/UA (Courtesy Kobal); p20 (t) Bodleian Library: Mal. 210. Dr. Faustus, 1631, title page woodcut; p20 (bl) Fortean Picture Library; p21 (t) K F Lord/Fortean Picture Library; p21 (bl) Guy Lyon Playfair/Fortean Picture Library; p23 Popperfoto; p27 MARY EVANS PICTURE LIBRARY; p29 (tl) MARY EVANS/HARRY PRICE COLL., UNIV. OF LONDON; p30 (tr) MARY EVANS/HARRY PRICE COLL. UNIV. OF LONDON; p31 (l) MARY EVANS/HARRY PRICE COLL., UNIV. OF LONDON; p31 (tr) Tim Jackson, Oxford Scientific Films; p33 (tr) Paranormal Picture Library; p33 (r) COMPAQ COMPUTER: Compaq's Multimedia Presario 1615 notebook for the home user; p34 (l) Guy Lyon Playfair/Fortean Picture Library; p35 (tr) Dimitri Ilic, Comstock 1998; p36 Comstock 1998; p37 (r) Nigel Smith/Hutchison; p38 (r) Copyright 1976/1993 Larry E Arnold/Fortean Picture Library; p39 (bl) Tony Stone Images; p39 (b) Tony Stone Images; p39 (r) Tony Stone Images; p40 Paul Screeton/Fortean Picture Library; p42 (bl) Mick Sharp photography; p43 (bl) MARY EVANS PICTURE LIBRARY; p47 *Fortean Times* Magazine.

With thanks to Zöe Wray and Linda Penny